Facing the Worst Case Scenario

Maerlis leaned forward, holding the comm in her lap. "I know we're a fresh food outpost, so I hate to ask. What happens to our supplies in that time?"

"Considering that the freighters won't bring a damn thing with them?" Jim said. "Besides what little we can't grow here. Even if we warn them, they won't likely be able to detour to another supply planet."

"There aren't any other ones close by." Rob's face was as pale as it had been flushed.

"Not that they could re-route to." Jim scrubbed his face. His brain didn't want to see the answer, much less say it out loud. "We won't actually starve to death. At least I don't think so. You'll know the nutritional deficiencies we'll run into better than I do, Maerlis, with a year or more before we get a good harvest. But we'll have a planet full of miserable cadets and furious miners on our hands."

Jim kept his true worries, and his memories, to himself. He'd seen people as rough and hardened as the miners on a desolate planet. At the end of the last wars on Earth.

He knew how more shortages and hardships they weren't prepared for could turn a difficult situation into a nasty one.

To my Dad, Jim Steffey

*For his incredible ability to grow anything,
his love of helping people,
and his endless curiosity.*

RESTRICTED SPECIES

KARI KILGORE

SPIRAL PUBLISHING, LTD.

CHAPTER 1

Jim Turhan couldn't quite remember why he'd started his nighttime habit of strolling around his cadet training lab on Mossera 4. He rarely saw another living creature, human or otherwise. No one wandering through empty xeno-botany classrooms or huddled in front of a holo-comm, homesick and lonely. Even when he looped outside into the crop supply planet's dim twilight, Jim was alone.

Jim had no doubt the rotating groups of ConSpace recruits got homesick all the time. Most were so young, humans still in their teens, aliens in the same awkward, confusing life stage. None of them were from the neighborhood or within a month's travel. Even with great clusters of stars close enough to leach darkness from the night sky, the Mossera System was as far from habitable worlds as you could get without a few years of hyper-sleep.

The structure and schedule for first year cadets at the Mosslea Academy focused on one thing. Keep them just overwhelmed and exhausted enough that they won't have time or energy to get into trouble. Sure, they'd retain a good bit of what they learned in their weary brain cells, and they'd make lifelong friends along the way. Those were side benefits.

Keeping them out of mischief until they grew some common sense was the only way to end up with graduates rather than washouts. Or worse.

Passing the outermost rows of octo-triticale, Jim brushed his hand across the waist high plants, faintly brown and green in the twilight. Wispy tassels and spiky rows of seeds tickled his palm and wrist. The nutrient-packed wheat seemed to thrive no matter where humanity scattered their seeds, even on a planet with no native pollinators or any other kind of insect.

Jim was mostly glad they only had the pollinator drones he specialized in, ranging from barely visible midge-bots to metallic hummingbirds. He'd read about the biting, stinging kind that died out on Earth before he was born.

Mossera 4 had no life forms that weren't firmly rooted in the ground. And everything turning this formerly wet but lifeless hunk of rock into a lush farmworld came from some-where else.

He followed the faintly glowing plas-rock path that crunched under his feet, back toward the academy's domes powered down to essential lighting and systems. Jim could easily make out the rounded roofs of greenhouses and square classrooms. A breeze funneled between buildings carried the scent of rosemary bushes after the day's rainstorm. He hardly ever worked in the herb sector, but Jim never grew tired of those surprise bursts of aroma.

Mosslea wasn't a lively entertainment region, not like Mosserrania, the leisure continent around the warm equatorial zone of Mossera 4. ConSpace usually did their best to pair up supply and leisure when they sent miners into less than hospitable conditions.

Mossera 5, the ore- and energy-rich planet every operation on 4 supported, fit that definition better than most. Well below freezing, almost non-existent atmosphere, no water to speak of.

Jim had never set foot on the arid, treacherous orange and black surface, much less beneath in the kilometers of mines. He had no desire to change that. All he needed to know about 5 was ConSpace needed those resources enough to dedicate an entire planet to supporting those miners.

A faint, bluish light inside the pollinator drone lab pulled Jim out of his visions of the hellish landscape barely two hundred million kilometers away. Every light system in the lab complex powered down automatically for evening, powering up only if someone triggered it.

Only one other resident would possibly be wandering around so late into sleep hours. And working, at that.

Sure enough, a head full of spiky blond hair was visible in the drone assembly and maintenance section. Rob Martinez leaned over one of the oval tables adjusted as high as it would go, elbows sunk into the pale blue moss surface just like when he was a raw cadet more than ten years ago. He'd finally grown into his lanky arms and legs, and into his quick and sometimes troublesome mind, turning into the natural xeno-farmer Jim suspected he'd be.

Not that it wasn't a near thing for a while there. Rob's struggle to believe in himself had been long and painful to watch.

"You authorized to be in here alone, kid?" Jim said, smiling when Rob's head popped up.

"Someone's gotta keep the place organized. The old man in charge keeps wandering off in the middle of the night."

Jim snorted as he joined Rob at the table. Seemed silly to call a man in his early thirties a kid. Looking back from pushing eighty himself made just about everyone seem like a kid. Lifespans and medical advances, not to mention living several decades on such a pure, clean planet meant he likely had a good forty years ahead of him.

The kilometers added up though, especially from when he was younger than Rob.

War years always seemed to add double.

"Night's the only time I can get some peace and quiet around this place." Jim glanced at the drifts and piles of disassembled drones covering the flat blue surface. Moth, fly, maybe a honeybee or two. "Did the cadets break more than their usual quota today?"

"No more than usual, no. I doubt any of them could come close to my personal record." Rob ran his hands through already messy hair, a habit from his challenging cadet years. "Wish it was something that easy to deal with."

Jim brushed the surface of the moss, smoothing some of the divots his former troublesome student still made. The moss not only helped keep the air clean and smelling more like a hardwood forest after the rain instead of nervous sweat. All the pollination drones, from nearly invisible midges up to dive bomb hummingbirds, were programed to land there in case they got away.

They always got away from new cadets. Every single time.

"What's going on?"

Rob picked up an empty pollen sack from one of the mechanical honeybees. The rice grain-sized pouches were soft transparent poly-plas. Or at least they should have been transparent. Some careless cadet, combined with careless supervision, had left these dusted with yellowish powder.

"These were last used a few days ago." Rob held the sack up toward the overhead grow-lights. The rubbery black wrist-mag he wore created the static field he needed for a good grip. "Put away a mess, as you can see."

"I know you're not out here late at night cleaning up after a bunch of sloppy cadets."

"Nope. I checked out the summer squash vines this afternoon. The ones we got a few years ago from old Earth stock? The plants look great, growing like wildfire. And not one blossom is setting fruit."

Jim scowled. "That can't be right. We ran those drones… well, a few days ago, just like you said. I watched your sloppy cadets load up the pollen myself."

"Same way you watched me load it up way back when, I know. I took the cadets out that day to see the drones in action since the squash blossoms are so big. Everything seemed normal. No heavy wind, no rain until yesterday."

"From the looks of these pollen sacks," Jim said, "they used up most of it out there. Even if they didn't bother to clean up." He picked up several of the sacks and shook them in his palm. The rattling motion rewarded him with a fine coating of yellow dust. "Anything strange about this batch?"

Rob straightened to his full height, several hands taller than Jim, stretching his arms above his head.

"Not that I can see. We collected it last season from the male blossoms. Standard procedure with a new strain."

Jim shivered, remembering his grandparents' tales of failed crops back on Earth. How they thought it was isolated at first, but the problem continued and spread. How waves of shortages and starvation led to conflicts that lasted long enough to catch Jim up in their final gasps of violence. Rapid colonization, and ConSpace developing the drones scattered in front of him, turned humanity's descent into triumph.

"We need to check the other crops," Jim said, dropping the cleaner pollen sacks and rubbing his palms on the table moss. "Have we sent any of this pollen out to other xeno-farms?"

"Not yet. We hadn't established our own supplies enough. This strain has grown true on at least a hundred other planets and moons. Think it could be a local problem? Soil or water, maybe?"

"That or some kind of problem we haven't seen before. Much as we screen out cadets from disease-prone planets and sterilize everything, we know something could get through. Got enough to keep the kids busy tomorrow?"

Rob grinned. "Already got it planned. Every single drone gets broken down and cleaned. Perfect opportunity to explain how problems spread without letting anyone know what's going on. And to watch the cadets who left this mess do it the right way."

"They won't soon forget you looming over their shoulders. Glad to help if you need it. It's been a while since I got to intimidate a bunch of lazy kids." Jim helped Rob sort the drones back into their proper bins. "Good call on keeping this quiet, too. If this is a simple fix, we don't want ConSpace breathing down our necks or causing a panic for no good reason."

"If it's not, we'll have done everything we can on this end." Rob clapped Jim on the shoulder. "Let's get them started cleaning first thing, then we'll check the rest of the new crops. Get some sleep, old man. Long day ahead."

CHAPTER 2

The nostalgic glow of instilling a bit of healthy respect into new cadets, along with a vital refresher about drone maintenance, faded before Rob and Jim finished inspecting the first five crops. Only Earth species failing would have been bad enough. But they found evidence of the same lack of fruit in the violet protein-rich cassamond fruit from Sitendra 8, pumpkin-sized blue citrus from Piddo 2, and rich, starchy gipla trees.

All perfectly healthy and normal plants, in fields kilometers away from each other. All loaded with multicolored blossoms that fell with very little fruit behind.

Jim tried to push the chill now deep in his gut aside as he landed the hoverpod. The sprawling apple orchard could have been on Earth itself judging by historical photos and primitive videos. Sturdy, compact trunks spaced evenly across the low covergrass landscape, each grafted with different species of planetary heritage apples. The blue tint of Mossera's sun threw everything off, but most of the trees displayed the unmistakable red and yellow of ripening fruit.

Those were all pollinated months before, though.

Mossera 4's long, slow orbital tilt—much more gradual than Earth's—combined with a closer orbit to make repeated crops possible. Most of the trees also had several branches with nothing but leaves. Only a few new apples dotted the dusky green with tiny pink or green fruitlets smaller than Jim's fingernail.

"When were these pollinated?" Jim said. He noted everything on his wrist-comm, but that was only out of habit. He never forgot anything that scared him this badly.

"These are the oldest so far. Three weeks from the drone pass." Rob shook the branch closest to him, sending pink and white petals to the already covered ground. Jim counted less than ten infant apples where dozens should have been thriving. "What the hell is going on here?"

They'd walked the rows of every other crop, collecting samples of the flowers and making sure they had a clear picture of the damage. This time, Jim was relieved Rob didn't seem to have the heart for it either.

"I haven't seen or heard of anything like this, not even when Earth failed. That was gradual, such a slow decline that people didn't pay attention until it was too late."

"No disease I've read about hits several unrelated crops at once like this, either." Rob leaned against the curved glass bubble of the hoverpod. "The drones should be able to pollinate these apples without our help, really. The orchard is decades old. We just load the pollen to get a better yield these days."

"That's what we're seeing, Rob. We probably would have had better results if we'd sent out empty drones. We're going to have to check the pollen stores. Maerlis Quan has a group of students studying diseases, doesn't she?"

The younger man's cheeks flushed pink, and he studied his fingernails intently. Jim tried to hide his smile. He hadn't caught the signs before, but now that he thought about it…

"She does, yeah. I think she might be willing to help."

"I'll leave you to discuss it with her, maybe over lunch," Jim said. Rob's face turned nearly as dark as the reddest apple in the orchard, but to his credit, he looked Jim in the eye. "I'll gather pollen from every crop we inspected and meet you in her xeno-lab."

CHAPTER 3

Jim wished the trouble with the crops were as easy to diagnose as Rob and Maerlis. The xeno-biologist was as friendly and outgoing as Rob, but the two of them acted positively standoffish once Jim arrived. They were a perfectly matched set as far as he could tell.

Both strong and healthy, around the same age. Maerlis was as small and compact as Rob was tall and lanky, with waves of gleaming black hair falling loose past her shoulders. Both loved the odd combination of planetary isolation and intense socialization of repeated swarms of new cadets and departing graduates.

And each almost embarrassingly smitten with the other.

Rob's gaze followed Maerlis as she gathered equipment and supplies from around her compact lab, all gleaming plas-steel and flawlessly clean glass. The orderly straight lines of cabinets, storage and freezer units, and counters made the curvy, organic chaos of the drone section seem like a slow moving disaster.

If they couldn't isolate whatever was causing so many crops to fail, that might turn out to be true.

"Rob tells me you have samples of affected pollen and the sterile flowers?" Maerlis said, stopping in front of Jim. She glanced at Rob for an instant, but she hid her blush better than he did. "We'll see if it could be the pollen and not something else."

Jim handed palm-sized black sample pods directly to her rather than risking touching the spotless surfaces. Each carried a digital code identifying the source and age of the pollen or flowers inside. She dropped them one by one into a slot Jim hadn't noticed on what he thought was a shiny black cabinet along one wall. Maerlis must have noticed his raised eyebrows.

"This tests the chemical composition of each sample. It reads the code on the way down. If we have a mismatch, we'll know in a few seconds."

"Does it check DNA?" Jim said, stepping over for a closer look at the silent machine. "In case there's some kind of hybridization going on?"

"You'd think she'd have that equipment here, wouldn't you?" Rob's face was flaming red again, and he looked like he wanted to inhale the words back out of the air.

Jim had the clear impression the kid had just spilled the nerdiest pillow talk of all time.

"That *is* something I've discussed with ConSpace," Maerlis said. She smiled openly at Rob, apparently deciding to drop what little façade they had left. "The technology is cheap and fast these days, but it's not considered any kind of mission priority. This scanner will catch anything we should be worried about, they say."

"And ConSpace considers hybridization a good thing if it happens," Rob said. "If it helps crop adaptation to the planet, so much the better. If not, we go back to our pure pollen stores and that takes care of it."

"Exactly." Maerlis touched a flat yellow button in the

middle of the scanner, and a huge screen filled with blue letters. The data took up the whole wall, as long and tall as Jim's arm. "We check nutritional content, potential toxins, digestibility. No need to waste our time worrying about genetics. ConSpace has that handled, right? At least officially."

Jim stepped closer to the screen on one side, Rob on the other. Jim was no chemist or biologist, but he could read the species names and varieties with no trouble. Maerlis confirmed his impression before he could speak.

"Nothing unexpected here, Jim. According to this, every single grain and petal come from the species you coded onto the sample. We've got some other kind of problem."

Maerlis leaned against the table behind her, giving Jim and Rob the cue to do the same.

"I don't understand this then," Rob said, shaking his head. "Any chance of an airborne fungus or even an insect?"

Maerlis shrugged. "Not a trace of pathogen from what you gave me. I can't imagine insect life spontaneously evolving since we arrived here."

"And we sterilize anything before it comes to the surface," Jim said. "Cadets, visitors, miners, or anything they receive."

"What's next, Maerlis?" Rob said. "Send these off-planet for testing?"

She sighed and pushed herself away from the table. Jim and Rob followed her into a tiny office off the lab. Jim was amused to see her desk and the table behind it were as disorderly as the lab had been neat.

"Have a seat and I'll check the freighter schedule." Maerlis sat behind the drifts of equipment, sheets of slippery plas-paper, and several honest-to-goodness printed and bound books. She retrieved a flat touchscreen comm from the mess. "I'm pretty sure it won't be what you want to hear."

After a moment of touches and swipes, the xeno-biologist looked up with a half-smile.

"I'm afraid I was right. No ore pickups or supply deliveries for about five months. And all those ships are already inbound."

"So they won't have emergency supplies or testing equipment," Jim said. The chill had settled into his bones. "And we can't send anything out for what, at least a month or two after that?"

"At the soonest." Maerlis leaned forward, holding the comm in her lap. "I know we're a fresh food outpost, so I hate to ask. What happens to our supplies in that time?"

"Considering that the freighters won't bring a damn thing with them?" Jim said. "Besides what little we can't grow here. Even if we warn them, they won't likely be able to detour to another supply planet."

"There aren't any other ones close by." Rob's face was as pale as it had been flushed.

"Not that they could re-route to." Jim scrubbed his face. His brain didn't want to see the answer, much less say it out loud. "We won't actually starve to death. At least I don't think so. You'll know the nutritional deficiencies we'll run into better than I do, Maerlis, with a year or more before we get a good harvest. But we'll have a planet full of miserable cadets and furious miners on our hands."

Jim kept his true worries, and his memories, to himself. He'd seen people as rough and hardened as the miners on a desolate planet. At the end of the last wars on Earth.

He knew how more shortages and hardships they weren't prepared for could turn a difficult situation into a nasty one. Rob seemed to read his thoughts.

"Any chance ConSpace Security out here could help us? With emergency supplies? I hate to say this, but having them more visible down here might help if things get really bad."

"They depend on us for supplies too," Jim said. "That's why the system is set up the way it is. We have backup supplies, untouched seed and pollen, multiple sources and formulas for keeping the soil healthy. We can design and build new pollinator drones if we have to."

"But when our whole purpose here is to provide food," Maerlis said, "no one plans for a link in that chain to break."

Jim's mind reeled, thoughts, images, feelings best left in the past storming through like a thousand drones released at once. The only idea he could grasp was a question.

"Maerlis, I don't want to offend you. But what you said, about ConSpace handling genetics. Officially."

"I'm right with you, Jim. This is more than unofficial, you know. It's completely unauthorized."

Rob drummed his fingers on his leg.

"You told me that thing is older than we are, Maer."

"I sure did." She slapped her hands against her own thighs, then grabbed the comm and got to her feet. "More like fifty Earth years, to tell the truth. But if it solves our problem, it's worth the risk."

She paused to eject the sample pods from the scanner and drop them into Jim's bag. The two men followed her out into the echoing corridor, empty with all the available cadets pulled into drone sanitizing duty. Jim held his questions and tried to still his panic-tinged thoughts as they turned toward the residential pods.

They didn't follow any sort of gender or species divisions, but general planet seniority arrangements had grown up over time. Jim lived in the oldest section, adjacent to the working facilities. Maerlis and Rob were further out, almost in the cadet wings.

Maerlis led them into a cozy pod neither as neat as the lab nor as messy as her office. Jim would call it comfortable and lived in, and Rob obviously would, too. He headed toward a small door to the left of the living area before he realized what he was doing. This time he added pulling his hand back from the doorknob to his flushed face.

"I doubt we fooled Jim for a second," Maerlis said, laughing. "Go ahead."

"We don't have nearly enough families on this planet," Jim said. "Assuming we make it through the next year, I'm delighted for both of you."

Rob had the grace to simply open the door and stand aside for Maerlis and Jim to enter.

The room beyond wasn't much more than a closet. A few shelves were jammed with more of the ancient bound books and clothing for the various climates on Mossera 4. A small, scarred wooden table along one wall held a black box, nearly a meter on each side. Jim could tell it was electronic from dormant lights and touchscreens all over it. He didn't doubt the bulky thing was nearly his own age.

"My great-grandmother gave it to me." Maerlis sat on a wooden chair that looked nearly as old. "She was a geneticist. Worked for ConSpace, like most of the rest of us. When her orbital lab upgraded gene sequencers, they let her take this hulk with her."

She touched a button flush on the top, and the machine started up. Jim hadn't heard anything whir like that for decades.

"How do you keep it running?" he said.

"She taught me how. She gathered up all the spare parts she could find, then asked around for what everyone else had. I've been repairing it since I was about twelve. I couldn't leave it behind when I came out here. Not much use on a planet with no native species, but I figured I might not be here forever. She gave me all these musty old genetics books, too."

She winked up at Rob, then pulled out the first sample pod.

"This won't be nearly as fast as the scanner in my lab." She picked up a thin, flat tool that Jim recognized from drone maintenance. The pick opened the pod as easily as it did one of the big drone casings. She handed the comm to Rob.

"I transferred all our results to this," she said. "I'll give you the code, you note it."

She turned to look at Jim, mouth drawn to one side.

"This is going to take days if I work randomly, and we probably need to move faster than that. Any ideas where I should start?"

"Find the code for the squash," he said. "The first ones we caught. That's all fresh seed and pollen from old Earth stock. We need to start there."

CHAPTER 4

Several hours later, well into Jim's usual nighttime strolling hour, they had results from three species of pollen and flowers. And not the normal results from the modern scanner.

Maerlis pushed the chair back and rubbed her eyes.

"Same thing as before. The flower is a perfect match. The pollen has several sequences altered. Every one related to reproduction."

"But no trace of a ConSpace marker, right?" Rob rubbed her shoulders, finally getting over his shyness around Jim. "How is that possible?"

All three of them stumbled back into the kitchen to pick at their half-eaten meals. Jim knew he wasn't the only one wondering how long fresh food would hold out.

"It shouldn't *be* possible," Maerlis said. "There are a few of these ancient sequencers around, sure. But the means to manipulate the DNA itself, to make specific changes like this, was taken out of private hands after the final bio-attacks on Fassey decades ago."

Jim remembered that war, the only one he knew of that

was more destructive than the last conflicts on Earth. Centuries-old fears and paranoia about genetically engineered weapons had surpassed imagination during those long years in the Fassey system. Turned out one species could indeed create a weapon that would completely annihilate another if they were willing.

The Drephana had been willing.

Maerlis stared out at the twilit fields. "There's no evidence of tampering at all. Yet the changes are almost identical. This has to have been done on purpose."

"But who?" Rob said. He'd taken up Jim's walking habit, but confined to the tiny living pod he was going in circles. His questions were too. "And why?"

"We're never going to get there without how," Jim said.

He sat forward, squeezing his temples with the heels of his hands. Something, fluttering around from his own schoolboy days. Whispering through too many years of memories.

"A restricted species," he said. Not as quietly as he thought.

"A restricted what?" Rob stood beside Jim, held tilted to the side. "Restricted how?"

"I can't remember," Jim said. "I'd bet your great-grandmother could have, Maerlis."

The xeno-biologist jumped up fast enough to spill her water.

"She would have, yes." She dashed back into the sequencer closet and came back out with the comm. "We have the next best thing here!"

Jim met Rob's gaze, but the younger man shook his head. Maerlis tapped on the screen a few times, waited, then tapped again. She looked up, her eyes fierce and bright. Jim knew in that second exactly how Rob felt when he fell in love with her.

"She's awake, come on. I would have woken her up anyway, but this is easier. Crithiens are beasts when they've been asleep."

"Crithiens?" Rob stood frozen, staring at the floor. "You mean Kayren?"

Maerlis was already standing by the open door.

"Of course, Kayren. No one in the Mossera System knows more about history than she does. No one in *any* system, short of an artificial, knows more than a Crithien."

Jim took a step toward the door, trying to force his anxious and weary mind to keep up.

"They have…"

"Multiple brains and eidetic memory, yes." Maerlis waved toward the corridor. "They make connections faster than any human can. Move if you're coming with me!"

The tone of her voice cut straight through to Jim's spinal nerves, and Rob's as well from the look of it. Both men got out the door as fast as they could.

CHAPTER 5

Kayren lived closer to Jim's section, as befitted the colony's history professor and historian. She'd settled with the first wave, as Crithiens often did. Their deep, broad memories had led them to careers as explorers, investigators, and on permanent system juries as well. Computers were wonderful devices, as far as they went. Organic brains, especially Crithien brains, were still by far the best in the galaxy at making connections.

Kayren was still young by her species standards at just over two hundred Earth years. She only had five segments, each holding one of her brain structures. Jim wasn't nearly as disturbed as the new cadets often were when meeting what looked like a gigantic soft-shelled insect for the first time. But he braced himself when Maerlis knocked on the door.

The historian's leathery abdomen was a glowing magenta, a sure sign that she was about to molt again. She still had recognizable facial features, though, her compound eyes not quite as indistinct as they would soon be.

Seven limbs, thin and sharp like an old Earth shellfish, moved her three meter long bulk easily. Her mouth parts, shaped eerily like a triangular beak, managed to imitate human speech quite clearly. The purring buzz was downright pleasant once you got used to it.

"You have a mystery for me, Maerlis? Greetings, Jim, Rob. Please come inside."

Kayren's lounge was long and low, curved to suit her body, but she had human chairs and a couch as well. She wouldn't leave her quarters again until she finished the messy process of shedding her too-small shell.

"Thank you for inviting us, Kayren," Maerlis said, sitting closest to the Crithien. "We need to ask you about a restricted species."

"What is the nature of the restriction?"

Everyone looked at Jim, including a dozen glittering compound eyes.

"I, uh, I think it had to do with genetic manipulation. I can't remember, maybe a travel restriction?"

Kayren closed all of her eyes, and Jim noticed Rob letting out a breath the same way he did. The respite only lasted a couple of seconds.

"You speak of the Dalsoria. They are restricted from travel, ever since the ban on genetic engineering in the private sector. There have been reports of smuggled groups, however. Dalsoria are simple creatures, not well-suited to deal with questions of morality."

"They've been found recently?" Rob said. He sounded fascinated despite his unease. "In inhabited systems?"

"They have," Kayren said. "ConSpace and other authorities keep such matters secret so as not to inspire more questionable behavior. But Dalsoria have been found as recently as nine Earth years ago."

"What are they used for?" Jim said.

"Often blackmail, often against the larger corporate

systems. Forcing others to bend to the criminal will. Or for espionage among governments."

"How would we…" Maerlis shook her head. "How are they found, Kayren? Are there signs?"

"Their own genetics are mutable, changeable. Your grandmother likely would have studied them before the restriction. The Dalsor homeworld has high levels of radiation from an unstable atmosphere. It's a large moon orbiting a gas giant, rather like the moons of Jupiter in the old Earth system. They never developed a stable genome as a result, as defense against the constant damage. This leaves their bodies changeable as well."

"Changeable how?" Rob said. He was pale, but his drawn brow showed how closely he was listening.

"They can adapt to almost any environment once they touch a creature native to that world. They slowly change shape, but never an exact match. Close enough in less advanced populations, but deeply disturbing in more advanced ones. The ability they had to develop to survive on such a dangerous and unstable homeworld gives them nearly unlimited flexibility wherever they are taken."

"How could they possibly alter DNA without technology?" Maerlis said. She chewed her bottom lip and stared off into space. "Without hundreds or thousands of generations for breeding, that's not possible."

"Not for humans, no," Kayren said. "Nor for any other known species. The Dalsoria always retain a porous section somewhere on their bodies. If the target species is small enough, they absorb them and make the adjustments. If the target is large, they can absorb only part. Something as small as a human hand or foot would be enough. The crucial addition is a sort of virus that spreads the modification throughout the entire body, and then the entire population."

Jim shivered, his earlier chill taking over *his* body, along with his heart and mind. If this spread on its own, they might never be able to recover without starting over.

With supplies they couldn't get until it was too late.

"Will you share what you're searching for with me, my friend?" Kayren said, extending a limb toward Maerlis. Jim couldn't stop himself from staring at the soft human hand in the grip of five pincers. "For my history?"

"Of course I will, Kayren. We may end up sharing this with the entire galaxy."

"You will need to search for genetic modifications," Kayren said, "but not complicated ones. The pattern, once successfully altered, rarely deviates with the Dalsoria. They are not good at covering their tracks."

"Where would we look for them?" Rob said. "The Dalsoria. If one were in Mosslea or somewhere else on the planet?"

Kayren slowly knotted all of her limbs together across her torso.

"They would be found in groups, at least three or four. They are warm water creatures from a volatile homeworld, unable to stand the coolness of most of Mossera 4. Dalsoria would only be found around the equatorial zone."

"Mosserrania." Jim shook his head, horrified and amazed at the simplicity of the thing. "Where aliens and humans aren't paying attention to anything related to science or survival."

Kayren tilted her upper segment forward in a clear imitation of a human nod.

"Indeed. A place designed for relaxation and pleasure, but with vast unspoiled natural waterways would be ideal."

Maerlis stood, followed by Jim and Rob. Jim wasn't sure if his lightheadedness was because of the late hour or all the puzzle pieces swirling into place in his brain.

"Thank you, Kayren," Maerlis said, gripping the

Crithien's limb again. "I apologize for leaving so quickly. I promise to share everything we learn with you."

"I trust that you will, Maerlis. One more thing you must know. When searching for the shelter of Dalsoria who want to remain hidden, the acidic balance of the water is key. They excrete base rather than acid. The water nearby will be soft and sweet."

CHAPTER 6

JIM KEPT the quick pace with Maerlis and Rob, but his thinking was considerably slower. It was one thing to walk around late at night, letting his mind wander and his body relax. Trying to force his brain into mystery solving mode without at least a few hours of rest wasn't going to end well.

Thankfully Rob spoke up before Jim figured out how to, and before they got all the way back to the newer quarters.

"Listen Maer. I want to figure this out and I know Jim does too. But we've all got to get some rest."

She kept charging ahead with the same determined stride until Rob touched her arm. Jim saw her shoulders rise and fall in a slow breath before she turned.

"I don't think I *can* sleep. Not with starvation hanging over our heads. And all these kids…"

"If you don't mind a little detour," Jim said, "I believe I can help with that. Remember the fulmenberry fruit, Rob? You had that a time or two, back when you were a scared, green cadet."

Rob shook his head and laughed under his breath.

"Every night for a couple of months." He put his arm

around Maerlis. "I wouldn't have made it through my first cycle without Jim here. You never saw a more pathetic, homesick cadet in your life."

"I doubt that," she said, smiling at up Rob. "I've known a few sad cases."

"Well, don't send them all my way at once." Jim turned toward his quarters, willing to bet the lovebirds would follow him. "I can only grow so many fulmenbushes in a season."

One corridor over and three doors down brought them to Jim's home for most of his adult life. As often happened when he had company younger than himself, he was shy about opening the door. Not because of clutter, but because of lack of it.

Everyone old enough to remember the last Earth Wars tended to fall into one of two patterns. They either hoarded everything, surrounding themselves with more supplies and belongings than anyone could possibly need. Or they lived with the bare minimum for human survival.

Jim fell squarely into the latter group. He'd never wanted much besides the standard issue equipment, either as a soldier or as a teacher. Blank tan walls, a brown sofa and two matching chairs. Bare floors made of nearly indestructible strips of bamblewood. Even his kitchen and wardrobe were spare and easy to maintain. A couple of plates, bowls, and utensils. Several of exactly the same pants and shirts.

Neither Jim nor anyone else who remembered those difficult times found his empty quarters depressing or sad, any more than they found the cramped quarters dirty or undisciplined. Jim thought of each response as a way of making sure you always had enough.

You either got attached or detached.

"Same old Jim," Rob said, softening his words with a smile. "Can't lose what you never had in the first place."

"You got it. Come on through to the greenhouse. I have a fresh batch drying out there now."

The one well-supplied, even crowded, area of Jim's quarters was the huge greenhouse space. He'd picked this apartment not for the windows looking out over the fields, but for the chance to have his own miniature test lab. Four rows across and several of his strides long, the plas-glass enclosed room was still fragrant and warm even so late into the night cycle.

Jim did test new drone designs out here, and he sometimes tested new crop strains. But he loved this room for the same reason he'd wanted this assignment when the war was over.

The peace and calm of growing things

An unknown threat to that calm all over the planet terrified him to his bones.

"Did they model the big grow houses on this one?" Maerlis said. She stopped and peered at every new group of plants in the waist-high row.

"More the other way around. They had the big ones started before I got here. I just wanted somewhere to putter."

The fulmenbushes grew along the back row, perpendicular to the rest. They were nearly a meter high, covered with deep orange leaves nearly as big as Jim's hand all season long. The berries, huge and bright green and shiny, sprouted all along the trunk and branches.

"I'll spoil a bit of Jim's fun," Rob said, taking Maerlis's hand. "Don't let him convince you to try one of the fresh ones. They're bitter enough to make your throat hurt, right before your whole mouth goes numb for a couple of hours."

"You never tried anything without knowing exactly what it was after that, did you?" Jim pulled a heavy metal tray from the row under the bushes. The lights down there left the tray warm, but not too hot to handle. "They dry up sweet, and the concentrated fruit works a lot better."

The shriveled berries were much smaller, about the size of old Earth blueberries. He dropped one into each outstretched hand.

"Only one," Rob said, nodding to himself. "More than that, and you'll wake up with a hell of a headache. Not to mention your guts get plugged up tight for a couple of days."

Rob's face flashed red when he met Maerlis's eyes, and she burst into laughter.

"I'll keep that in mind. Thanks, Jim. Late breakfast at my place?"

"I could use that extra hour or two of sleep," Jim said. "We just have to figure out an excuse to run off for a vacation."

CHAPTER 7

Just as Jim had expected, Rob was already with Maerlis when she opened her door the next morning. And Rob hadn't yet changed out of his brown robe, made extra long to suit his height. Maerlis at least was fully dressed and ready for the day, and handed Jim a cup of coffee before he could say a word.

"I tested a few samples from the pollen stores," she said, walking back to her small kitchen table. "While Rob was still snoozing. The sealed ones are fine, no mutations. Whatever happened was outside those secured units."

"Thank goodness for that," Jim said. He drained half his coffee in one steaming hot gulp. "At least we know where the problem is *not*. Kayren said whatever the Dalsoria touch spreads like a virus, though. If it is them, we'll have a challenge getting everything cleaned up again."

"We have to work out a good way to get to Mosserrania first," Rob said. He had a nearly empty cup of coffee in front of him, and an empty plate and bowl. "Shuttles leave every couple of hours even this time of year. We just need a reason we can admit to."

"Got that covered." Jim helped himself to a bowlful of hot porridge, with orange and red fruit from last harvest. He hoped it wasn't the last for a while. "I woke up thinking about how we're always wanting to establish a larger food growing area around the equatorial zone. Things we can't grow in Mosslea outside of the greenhouses."

"Sure," Maerlis said. "We could all use more fresh fruit. But they're not going to give up enough of the leisure zone for something as unexciting as food."

"Probably not," Jim said. "But that doesn't stop us from going down to consult. They actually do want us to manufacture drones for them, to pollinate their flowers and enough fruit for the resorts to use."

Rob snorted. "Yeah, the decorative drones I keep hearing about. Jewel tones to match each resort's colors. They even want each set to buzz in a different key so they can tell them apart. Last time I checked, how well the drones work matters a lot more than how pretty they are."

"Silly as it sounds," Jim said, "this all works to our advantage. No one knows more about drone design than we do. And Maerlis here would be the best choice for making sure all these new exotic fruits don't cause contamination with our existing crops."

"You think ConSpace will go along with this?" Maerlis had cleared her own place except for what looked like a very cold cup of coffee.

"They already have," Jim said, grinning. "Our shuttle leaves in three hours. That enough time for you two to get packed and ready?"

CHAPTER 8

THE CONSPACE EMPLOYEE shuttle was hardly luxurious, certainly not compared to what occasional tourists or the wealthier long-term miners were treated to. Jim, Maerlis, and Rob sat on uncomfortable, barely padded seats rather than recliners with cushions that felt like a massage. They were free to bring their own drinks or snacks for the two-hour trip, but they wouldn't have attendants and menus to choose from. Of course a cost of free made minimal accommodations a lot easier to accept.

Best of all, the odd travel day and travel season meant they had the small, boxy aircraft to themselves. Not even a human pilot to worry about hearing them.

Jim already expected Maerlis to be the best prepared of all of them, and she didn't let him down. Her palm-sized touchscreen was loaded with everything she could find about Dalsoria, their abilities, and their restrictions. He suspected Kayren and her advanced security clearance had helped.

Even the most hidden data wouldn't say how they were possibly going to locate a banned species on a vast, unfamiliar continent.

"This is tragic, really," Maerlis said. "Dalsoria never have understood the trouble they've caused, or the trouble they're in. Genetic modifications are as natural as breathing to them. Their biggest flaw is they trust strangers far too easily."

"I'd never even heard of them," Rob said.

Jim shrugged. "You wouldn't have. They were restricted long before you were born. I had no idea they'd cropped up so recently. You can imagine how often that would happen if they were better known."

"But why?" Maerlis said. She put the screen on the table between them. "Why target us like this? An agricultural post is about as far from warlike as it gets."

"Sure, down here," Jim said. "But remember what we support. ConSpace isn't the only player when it comes to resource extraction or transport. Kayren didn't mention corporations, but she mentioned espionage and governments. ConSpace is bigger than any planetary government, and wealthier than most systems."

"They have to have made enemies along the way," Rob said. "Just going by their public history, much less what never gets passed along to us farmers. Are you sure this is something we can handle? Shouldn't we bring in ConSpace for something this dangerous?"

"I thought a lot about that this morning," Jim said. "Even started to do just that. Have you ever had to call them in, Maerlis? To solve a problem before you understood what was going on yourself?"

She swore under her breath, turning toward the window.

"A teacher of mine did, once. An unknown disease on a new colony. They charged in and took over everything. By the time they were finished, the native populations were nearly wiped out. Most of the early colonists were, too, mainly from panic."

Jim frowned and nodded at the same time.

"That's what I've found, too. Once I know what's going on and what I need, ConSpace is the most powerful ally in any system. Before that, they're the most destructive force. I'm afraid we'd have a panic down here and up on Mossera 5."

The three of them fell silent, watching a vast desert wasteland underneath their shuttle. Jim knew ConSpace had hopes of bringing this arid continent into food and resource production to support the miners someday. Assuming the colony lasted that long

"I hate to sound like a warning loop," he said, "but we're getting ahead of ourselves. Knowing *why* won't help us. Not yet. If Kayren is right, we have to find these creatures first."

"Have you ever known a Crithien to be wrong?" Maerlis said, smiling. "I haven't spent much time on Mosserrania. Either of you know how we might find them?"

Rob shrugged, shaking his head.

"I haven't been there much," Jim said. "Not for a long time. An old buddy dragged me down there, a couple of months after I got here and before he shipped back out. He was a lot more into the entertainment side of things than I was by then. I spent most of my time…"

Both Rob and Maerlis responded to Jim's slow smile.

"Spill it, old man," Rob said.

Maerlis picked up her tablet, ready to search.

"I spent most of my time getting to know everyone who was already here. Everything, too. There's a delightful species we need to seek out. Greponians might be just who we're looking for."

"They…they're like giant old Earth sea otters," Maerlis said, grinning like a little girl. Rob's expression matched as soon as she held up the tablet.

"Violet sea otters?" he said.

"That's the ones," Jim said. "They work as entertainers, and they're whip smart. Funny, too. I bet they'll jump at the chance to do something different."

"Kind of like we did," Maerlis said.

CHAPTER 9

Mosserrania was as carefully designed and engineered as anything else ConSpace invested in. Visitors could always find what they sought, but they were never confronted with anything else. A family with small children wouldn't accidentally wander into a gambling palace, or a resort devoted to adult entertainment. And no adults would be forced to wander through pastel fairy tale landscapes when they sought only more mature activities.

There was no need for such surprises, not with a string of vast islands circling the planet, each dedicated to a specific sort of recreation.

What Jim and his friends sought waited in the middle of one of the larger family complexes, only a short air-bus ride from the main arrival terminal. The flat, sandy expanse had been converted into a water park. Bright, open buildings surrounded warm lagoons and bays, all sculpted and maintained to child-friendly perfection.

The natural greenish sand remained around the outskirts, with pastel beach houses lining the shore. Inland, the sand changed to sky blue, lavender, pink, every cheerful shade with buildings and walkways to match. The heady floral scents from flowers in every possible shape and size were overwhelming compared to the more mundane vegetal smells Jim was used to.

Jim understood Rob's annoyance at something mistaking their vital drones as coordinating toys, but he thought jewel-colored versions would be lovely flying through the wild varieties of plants and flowers. Not to mention a great way to educate miners and tourists alike on the critical work of the farming zone and Mosslea Academy.

Work that was well on the way to disaster if they couldn't figure out why crops were failing.

The busier season on Mosserrania matched the cycles of the mining planet they supported, like all of Mossera 4. Gigantic ConSpace freighters had departed a few weeks earlier, loaded with several months' worth of precious ores and metals. Now with the new extraction cycle underway, only a few off-system tourists wandered in a vacation daze.

Jim, Maerlis, and Rob ignored the temptation of warm water and nearly deserted beaches, heading instead for the performance areas in the middle of the island. A deep, vast pool lined in warm gold tones, surrounded by rows of tiered seating, served as the professional home for many of the water performers.

"This place is beautiful and all," Maerlis said, staring at the rows of palm trees behind the seating area. Their broad leaves and trunks ranged from palest pink and blue to deep burgundy and indigo. "But no one's here. Are any Greponians around?"

"They take their vacations when the miners get back to work," Jim said. "But they usually have a show once a week or so for the off-worlders. I put in a call before we left to see if one of them could speak to us."

A ripple broke the surface of the perfectly clear water,

and a violet streak crossed from the opposite side of the pool. Jim's eyes couldn't track the speed, but he knew what was coming. Rob and Maerlis gasped when a fuzzy head bigger than a human's splashed up by their feet.

The Greponian was the largest and oldest Jim had ever seen, easily twice his own size. The fur around its mouth, eyes, and most of its face had faded to black, covering up the distinctive coppery markings that made it easy to tell individuals apart.

Her mouth, he amended, when he caught sight of her elongated deep blue fangs. He didn't know the specialized teeth could extend so far, nearly past the creature's rounded chin.

A clear reminder that while the giant violet otters seemed friendly and joyful during performances, and they usually were with tourists, they were also fierce hunters and fighters.

Jim slipped a tiny translation bud into his ear, noticing the Greponian already wore a water-proof version in her flat, oval ear opening. Rob and Maerlis did the same.

"Greetings to you, ma'am," he said. "Thank you for taking the time to speak with us."

She regarded the three of them with deep green eyes, then shook herself. She took care not to spray water onto the humans, unlike during a performance. Her voice sounded like a range of low-pitched growls and barks to his open ear.

"No one calls me ma'am but the wretched pups I try to train some sense into. Junima will do."

Jim knelt on the warm, rough concrete, waiting while Maerlis and Rob joined him. Junima's rich aroma of fish and seaweed rose all around them.

"I'm Jim, this is Maerlis and Rob. We do our best to train cadets on Mosslea. You have my sympathy."

"Sympathy or not, you're keeping me from my work. What do you want from me, Jim?"

Her tone, even through the translator, reminded Jim of his commanders during the Earth Wars. Might as well get to the point, and hope she had more sympathy than they ever had.

"We won't keep you, Junima. You may know we've been working to expand food production into warmer climates. Hoping to grow more varieties of fruit and such."

Junima snorted water from around her dark purple nose.

"Enough of my pups already waste time working in the seafood facilities. No other species working for ConSpace is forced to take shifts growing their own food. We cater to the miners enough as it is."

Jim decided not to mention how many farmers labored to do exactly that.

"Nothing like that, no. We just need to scout for a specific location, one we think the Greponians can help us find."

"This whole blasted planet has been mapped," Junima said. "Every inch of the land and sea. You want to go exploring, find another world."

"No ma'am," Maerlis said. "Junima, I mean. It's not something we can see on a map. We seek a certain type of water environment."

Junima heaved half of her torso out of the water, this time not bothering to be careful of the splash. Her four back legs, webbed into great flippers, stayed under. Her front feet, with six fingers ending in curved black claws, flexed on the concrete.

Rob and Maerlis stood and took a step back, but Jim stayed put. Junima's eyes, and fangs, were inches from his face now.

"Seems you don't train your pups all that well, Jim. They don't even know not to speak out of turn."

"Maerlis and Rob are leaders themselves, no longer

cadets." Jim put a hand on Rob's knee, trying to keep him from coming forward. "All we ask is to work with some of your most mature pups for a couple of days. I know they'll be more than well-trained enough to help us."

"They're not trained to do any such thing. They don't have to be. Unlike humans, Greponians have more than enough senses and instincts for such simple tasks."

"So you'll help us," Maerlis said. Jim was proud of how her voice didn't even tremble.

Junima glared at her, then back at Jim.

"If ConSpace is actually supporting this nonsense, I don't have much choice. Just show me your authorization, and I'll decide how to proceed."

"Our travel auth is right here," Rob said, reaching into his pocket.

"I don't need to see a damn travel auth." Junima flipped her broad tail, sending ripples through the pool. "You couldn't even get down here without that. Show me the ConSpace authorization for my pups to search for your special water. Or, tell me what you're actually after."

Jim didn't need the translator to know this wasn't going to work. Junima had the trick of narrowing her eyes perfected as well as any human commander. They were going to have to find another way.

"Unless I miss my guess, ma'am," he said, "you have enough military or government experience to know we can't share the details of every mission. ConSpace approved our travel. They did not approve my sharing the details of what we're here to do."

"Right. Likely because they don't know. You've wasted enough of my time, and you won't be wasting any of my pups' time. If you bother any of us with this nonsense again, I'll report all of you. Then we'll see who knows what."

Jim stood and pulled the others back just as Junima submerged, sending a wave rushing over the edge of the pool.

"Great," Rob said, stomping water off his boots. "Nice manners on that one. Glad she wasn't my teacher when I was a pup."

"We can't risk telling her what's really going on," Jim said. "She'd go right to ConSpace Security."

Maerlis stepped to the edge of the pool and leaned forward, looking into the still agitated water.

"Any other ideas how we can find the Dalsoria? From what Kayren said, they're going to be pretty well hidden."

"Not yet," Jim said. He thought he heard soft ripples in one of the smaller pools behind them, but he didn't see anything moving. "Not without causing exactly the panic we need to avoid. The only thing worse than food shortages would be telling anyone we have a restricted species loose on the planet."

CHAPTER 10

A MEAL rich with the seafood Junima's pups helped maintain and a long conversation afterward left them no closer to a solution. The hotel's elaborate fairy tale decorations, sparkling light fixtures, and overly attentive service felt decadent after years spent in Mosslea's utilitarian spaces.

Jim enjoyed watching the young couple marvel at everything, but it made him uncomfortable. Especially with trouble he couldn't figure out how to solve hanging over his head, sinking into his tense shoulders.

Mossera's bluish sun set hours earlier than Jim was used to so close to the equator, but he knew he'd never be able to get to sleep so early. Not with his nighttime prowling habits on top of his worry.

He set out wandering the lush tropical landscape shortly after Maerlis and Rob retired for the night, wishing he'd brought a supply of dried fulmenberries with him. Lighted paths through the flowers and along the beach gave him more than enough to explore on an island that could easily accommodate a few thousand people. He hoped the mindless walking would let his mind relax and come up with something. Anything.

The warm sand felt good under Jim's bare feet and between his toes, almost as good as the soothing rhythm of waves sounded to his ears. Aching calves sent him back to the paths before long. He passed through a fruit picking area designed for children, gathering handfuls of everything he recognized. His favorite was tiny yellow starecks that started off tart enough to make his jaws ache, then turned sweet when he crunched them between his teeth.

He was sure someone in Mosserrania would have equipment that could test the water. There were too many aquaculture habitats set up and maintained for diving and other recreational uses, along with the underwater food production zones. But Jim knew anyone he talked to about using that equipment would be even more suspicious than Junima, and with good reason.

He headed toward the lagoons and pools, deserted and silent. He hadn't seen or heard from Junima after her abrupt departure. The possibility of a year without a good harvest wouldn't impact Greponians or any other species that depended on seafood nearly as much as it would everyone else.

At least not until ConSpace claimed everything they could to support the essential mining operations, leaving the rest to fend for themselves.

He stopped at the edge of the big performing pool, wondering if the soft light around the edges was organic or electric. The Greponians he'd spent time with years ago hadn't been nearly so grouchy or worried about rules and regulations. They'd been a lot more like his rowdy older cadets, willing and eager to get into trouble any chance they got.

Of course the ones he'd known had been around that

same age, not crusty old veterans like Junima. Or like he was now.

Jim spun around at the same ripple and soft splash he'd heard earlier. The small pool wasn't nearly as well-lit as the big one, but he could just make out a dark shape moving toward him. He fumbled in his pocket for his translator bud, pulling out the hotel-issue flashlight at the same time.

The Greponian floating at the edge didn't have a trace of black fur in the violet. The metallic coppery markings were clear and distinct, swirling around her eyes and cheeks like the ripples spreading away from her body. Her fangs only showed a few millimeters past her mouth, and she wasn't much bigger than Maerlis. Still, she stared up at Jim, bold and not bothering to hide.

"I'm sorry," he said, finally slipping the translator into place. "You startled me. I'm Jim."

"I did not mean to startle you, Jim." Her grunts and growls were higher and softer than Junima's. "I am Belles."

"Were you here earlier? When we were speaking to Junima?"

"I was. All these pools are connected by tunnels. I was finished with my practice drills and helping the younger pups. And I was bored. So I followed her."

Jim sat on the soft grass that surrounded the pool, grunting at how sore his hips and back were. He'd walked a lot more than he usually did tonight.

"I'm guessing you overheard what we were talking about."

"Of course I did. We long ago learned it's in our best interest to hear whatever Junima says. At least we can try to be prepared. Sounds to me like you're worried about something you didn't want to tell her."

Jim recognized the curiosity and defiance from his earlier

encounters with these delightful creatures in her voice and the way her whiskers twitched forward.

"And if I am?"

"Some of us aren't determined to follow *all* the rules," Belles said. "We might be able to help you."

"Not afraid of getting in trouble if she finds out what you're up to?"

Jim recognized the rising and falling hiss, a Greponian's version of laughter. Hope sparked and glowed in his belly for the first time since Rob showed him the messy drones.

"We're old enough to have vacation time, no matter what Junima thinks. We've earned it. I'm not about to tell her where we're going or why. Are you, Jim?"

Jim laughed himself then. No matter the decade or the species, cadets never truly changed. And this situation certainly warranted breaking a few rules.

"Not a word from me. Got a suggestion of where we could meet and talk a little more? See if this is something you really want to get mixed up in?"

"Unlike Junima, many of us enjoy our time in the aquaculture areas and the diving zones. I worked in a particularly lovely one last season. Humans seem to enjoy visiting as well. If you're comfortable with diving, I could meet you there."

Jim got to his feet a little more slowly than usual, but the weight in his heart had lightened considerably. At least they had a chance now. At least they could try *something*.

"We'll manage, I'm sure. Got a couple of friends as brave as you?"

Belles ducked her face under the water for a second. When she came back up, Jim was sure he saw her smiling.

"A few. As Junima says, we have instincts for such work already. We would be neglecting our training if we didn't exercise those as well as our performance muscles."

CHAPTER 11

BELLES WIPED out any lingering doubts Jim had about her willing participation before he woke up the next morning. Along with a message confirming a diving outing for himself, Rob, and Maerlis, they found all the equipment they'd need waiting in the hotel lobby.

The snorkels and goggles were decidedly old-fashioned, as were the long flippers. Even if they were in bright shades of green and yellow. The modern tech upgrade of ear and mouthpieces for communication and translation were welcome additions.

"We're not going to get Belles into trouble?" Maerlis said. They were all out front, dressed for the water, waiting for their Greponian escort and co-conspirator to arrive. "Sounds to me like she's just a kid. Junima doesn't seem like a good one to cross."

"She's young, sure," Jim said. He hoped his farmer legs weren't too painfully white in swim shorts. "But she's already working with younger pups of her own. And she came to me."

"She went through all the official channels to set this dive up," Rob said. "I doubt this is her first go round with bucking authority. She's better than I was at such things."

Maerlis rolled her eyes and took Rob's hand. Unlike the two men, she looked stunning in her bright red swimsuit, with muscles and curves in all the right places. Between that and her sharp intelligence and curiosity, Jim wondered if the younger man would be concentrating on anything besides her all day long.

"You're still not good at such things, Rob," she said. "I guess we're about to find out about the rest."

A low hum from the left warned them right before their diving tug came into view. Only a few paces across in either direction, the flat craft had rows of seating along all four sides. The space in the middle was open to the water.

Two sleek violet shapes bounded and splashed along just in front of the boat, with three more alongside. They all seemed around the same size as Belles, and Jim spotted three with visible female fangs. The humans walked along a short, vibrant pink dock to meet the pups.

"Good morning, Jim," Belles called. "My friends hope you don't mind if they accompany you on your dive. This is Suma, Alor, Nesil, and Tafen."

Each of the pups ducked their heads in turn. Jim grinned, noticing his friends doing the same.

"Not at all. Happy to meet all of you. This is Maerlis and Rob."

"We're ready to get underway, then." Belles swam in a quick circle around the boat, coming back up beside the dock. "This craft is already set to take us to my favorite diving area, only a few minutes away. You may sit or float in the tank, to get used to the water."

Maerlis immediately slipped into the water. Rob hesitated and moved slowly, but once he stood on the bottom of the tank, he seemed to relax. Belles and the one she'd called

Nesil joined them, while Jim got comfortable on one of the benches.

"Is such a close location the best choice for today?" Maerlis said. "With what we have planned?"

"It's perfectly fine," Belles said. "The rumor is Junima resents ocean duty because she's grown to hate the open water. I think she's been in the pools too long, myself."

The boat moved out, slow enough that Jim could have swam alongside and kept up. He noticed several small speakers just under the bench seats, probably for larger groups, and louder ones. The craft itself was nearly silent.

"How much do your friends know, Belles?" he said.

"As much as I do. I have to point out that that's not much of anything."

"No one knows besides the three of us," Rob said. "We could be in for some serious trouble over the next several months."

"Whatever you say is safe with us, Rob," the male called Nesil said. His copper markings streaked like lightning away from his nose and eyes. "We've kept plenty of secrets for a long, long time."

Jim shared what he knew, pausing to let Rob and Maerlis add as much as they could. By the time they arrived at the dive site, a wide, perfect circle of multicolored sand with trees and bushes to match, all the Greponians had fallen silent. Instead of splashing and jumping, they swam quietly.

"I'm sorry to give you so much bad news." Jim stepped off the boat onto the hot lime green sand. "But we've got to find these Dalsoria as soon as we can, assuming that's what's happening."

"You have to be careful if you do find them," Maerlis said. "Don't touch them, no matter what else happens. Don't let them touch you. They don't mean to, but they can make you sick and spread it to every Greponian on Mossera 4."

"I only hope we can manage," Belles said, "in time to stop a disaster. When can we start?"

Rob blinked, then smiled at Jim. "We're ready right now. We just don't have any idea *where* to start."

"Do you know any of the coves and bays Kayren was talking about?" Maerlis said. "Quiet, isolated. Maybe with caves, and she said the water nearby would be soft and sweet."

The five otter-like creatures ducked under the water, heads close together. Jim couldn't hear a thing, but he was certain they were speaking too fast for human ears or electronic translators to keep up. After a couple of minutes, all five popped up at once.

"We can think of fifteen such areas," Belles said. "We'll probably find more when we can look at a map."

"Fifteen?" Jim rubbed at the back of his neck, trying not to get upset. Time was already desperately short. "How long will it take to search that many?"

"That depends on how much diving you plan to do on your vacation," Nesil said. "A few weeks, maybe five with what we have here. If you're enthusiastic enough to charter one of the big, fast hoverboats, though, the kind with warm water tanks built in, we could get that down to a few days."

Maerlis whistled. "You mean the kind a huge group usually rents. I'd love to dive off one of those things, someday when Rob finally lets me teach him how. But I can't afford one room, much less the whole thing."

"That's way above my pay grade," Rob said, shaking his head. "Even if I could swim."

"Don't know what I need a big retirement fund for anyway," Jim said. "It's not like I ever plan to quit. Starving to death isn't exactly the way I'd want to go out in any case. Make the arrangements, Belles."

Jim tried his best not to focus on the cost, or the weeks of vacation he could have bought instead. All the leisure time on Mosserrania or anywhere else wouldn't matter if the whole system collapsed, or if some kind of sinister outside group was responsible for the genetic modifications. Bad as the trouble already was, he was certain whoever this was wouldn't stop at interfering with their food supply.

All he could do was help map out the list of bays Belles and her friends gave them, and hope that list wouldn't get too much longer by the time they headed out in the morning.

No one back at the hotel had ever heard of fulmenberries. They were too rare for even a fully stocked leisure continent. But the human concierge gave all of them drinks to help them sleep without asking any questions.

Jim tried to remind himself to ask Belles if she'd had anything to do with that as he drifted off.

He fell sound asleep without his nighttime walk for the first time in decades.

CHAPTER 12

By the end of the second day of searching, the excitement and adventure had worn off for everyone. Even the young Greponians. Each cove was lush with human-seeded plants and grasses that didn't require specialized pollination. Each was pristine and beautiful, with no visible trace of habitation or even recent visits. Each remained empty, all the way to the back of every possible cave and habitat.

A few sites held faint remains of water that was sweeter than normal, lingering in the furthest reaches of the caves. Belles and Nesil felt sure that meant the Dalsoria must have been there. Neither they nor any of the other searchers had ever sensed water like that anywhere else on Mossera 4.

Those maddening clues didn't bring them any closer to locating the restricted species, or to understanding why they'd been altering the pollen stores.

Even the strange sense of exhilaration from being the only occupants on a glamorous vessel meant to host dozens of celebrating humans and performing Greponians wore thin. The boat was an engineering marvel, capable of sailing, cruising at typical air speeds over the water, and even closing up tight enough to fly faster than anything but ConSpace Security aircraft.

As sleek and modern as the family-style resort had been colorful and charming, their new home gave Jim, Maerlis, and Rob enough distractions to stay calm at first. The floors, walls, and ceilings were gleaming silver and black, accented with bright, angular artwork that changed throughout the day. Sails that glittered and changed color with every burst of wind towered overhead when they were moving slow. Maerlis in particular was fascinated with watching the moving parts as the ship shifted and transformed between different configurations.

The contract Jim signed stated in no uncertain terms that the three human crew members would be polite, respectful, and above all, discrete. The three women had given a tour of the ship, explained how the human diving equipment, small boats, and a miniature submarine functioned, and disappeared. Jim had to agree the crew were discrete, since he'd only caught sight of them when the ship dropped anchor or departed for a new location.

The full-body dive suits were far more advanced than the snorkel gear from a few days ago, and more than a little intimidating. Only Maerlis was enthusiastic about the equipment, trying all of it before the first day of searching was over.

Every failed search sent Jim further into worry about how much he was spending. Nearly a month's salary for every day that passed. And no matter how delicious the food was that they all enjoyed from the ship's stores, Rob spoke for everyone when he said every bite made him a little more fearful of the shortages to come.

As Mossera 4's blue-tinted sun headed toward the horizon on the second day, the ship waited still and quiet rather than shifting to its airborne configuration. Belles and

Nesil had organized their targets so they could sail or cruise at high speeds between locations during the day, then the crew would set the autonav overnight to their next destination. All five of the violet Greponians were still out searching.

Jim found Rob walking along the still-open deck, the first time he'd seen Rob without Maerlis since they'd left Mosslea. The set of the younger man's shoulders, the way he rubbed his thumbs back and forth over his fingertips as he walked, reminded Jim of the more difficult times of Rob's long ago cadet days.

"You authorized to be up here alone?"

Instead of turning, Rob only stopped walking. He gripped the transparent rail and stared out toward the open ocean. Whenever they were ready for flight, a similarly clear shield would drop for protection without blocking the view. But for now, the fresh salty breeze dried the sweat on Jim's face and neck.

"What are we doing out here, Jim? Every day we keep at it is another step toward some kind of food riots. Or these things we're looking for turning us all into some kind of mutants."

Jim stood beside him, watching the sunlight blazing on distant waves.

"What do you think we should be doing instead?"

"I think we should call this whole thing off and bring ConSpace Security in to handle it. Now, before the whole damn planet falls apart!" Rob took a deep breath, held it for a second, then turned to face Jim. "I'm sorry. I shouldn't have snapped like that."

"Don't you dare apologize. Not for speaking your mind when you need to. You may be right. It seemed like a good idea to try to figure this out ourselves when we started. I've been here way too long to deny that ConSpace functions a lot better when we bring them a solution ready to go. If a bunch of corporate types jump in and try to solve the problem before they understand it, a lot gets broken along the way."

"You sound just like Maerlis," Rob said. He smiled, but his features all turned down at once when he closed his eyes.

"Is she wanting to call them in, too?"

"Not even a little bit. She deals with them a lot more than I do, even more than you do. You heard what she said about trying to convince them to let her have simple gene sequencing equipment. She's wanting to get in the water and search herself."

He sighed, blowing air out through his lips. "She's none too happy with me right now, either."

Jim resisted a strong urge to put his arm around Rob's shoulders. What helped a scared teenager would probably upset or embarrass a grown man.

"First fight?" Jim said.

"No, we've had… Well, yeah. First real fight. First one that feels this bad."

"I won't pretend to give you relationship advice, since I don't have much to give. I do think you two are going to be just fine. I'm not going to ignore how you feel about this whole mess, either. Listen, we've got this thing hired for another two days. If we still come up empty, we'll all sit down and talk about what to do next. Okay?"

Rob focused on his hands for a couple of seconds, then he looked back up at Jim and nodded. Before either man could say more, a flurry of splashes and high-pitched squealing rounded the front of the ship.

Five violet streaks headed straight for the underwater portal and disappeared. By the time Rob and Jim raced down two flights of stairs to the tank level, Maerlis was already sitting cross-legged on the wet floor in front of the wall full of diving equipment.

"Slow down, the translator can't keep up," she said, holding both hands toward Belles. The other Greponians darted around behind the lead female, chattering and grunting to themselves. At least they'd stopped the ear-splitting squeals.

Belles looked up at Jim and Rob. Without turning, she raised her tail and hit the water with a huge, booming splash. The other four immediately stopped where they were and floated without a sound.

"No wonder she clashes with Junima," Rob said under his breath.

He stood beside Maerlis, rubbing his thumbs and fingertips again. When she held up her hand, he took it and sank to the floor beside her.

All five Greponians stared at Jim until he managed to sit on Maerlis's other side.

"Did you find it?" Rob said.

"Not the sweet water, no," Belles said. "We met a group of Greponians working on a bed of grasses, a green one we don't have on Grepon."

"Seaweed, maybe laver or nori," Jim said. "An old Earth delicacy."

"Yes, seaweed. I've worked in those beds many times. They're having a problem with their crop, too."

"It's not growing?" Maerlis said. "Even when they seed them?"

"Not like that," Belles said. "They have the same fertility rate as before. The problem starts when the grasses grow and mature. They don't grow the soft leaves. They remain tough and spiny."

"The parts we eat," Jim said. His head spun, catching his stomach up in the whirling feeling of motion. "The parts any of us eat."

"Any sign of disease?" Maerlis said. "Maybe problems with the water?"

Nesil moved beside Belles.

"None," he said. "They've been trying to figure this out for several days now."

"And they're hearing of similar problems from other groups," Belles said. "All in this region for now."

"But probably not for long." Rob moved closer to Maerlis and put his arm around her waist. "They've been here, the Dalsoria. How fast does the seaweed get to this stage?"

"This species grows very quickly," Belles said. "They're seeing trouble in plants only a few days old."

"They're *still* here," Jim said. "Still active. Our pollen was altered long before this. The only way I can think to survive a long crop failure in the farm zone is to turn to the oceans."

"Now that's going, too." Maerlis pounded her fist on her knee. "What the hell for? If they're making some kind of demands or threats, they're being awfully damn quiet about it!"

Jim leaned forward, trailing his fingertips in the warm water. He remembered the danger and suffering of war far too clearly, even from so long ago. He'd rather jump into the tank and let Belles hold him under than see a peaceful world go through that again.

"They're not finished," he said. "Whoever's behind this. They want to make it clear how much power they hold before we ever find out what they want. If we can't figure this out and stop it, I'd bet they'll hit every food source we have. Probably fresh water, too."

"Should we…" Rob glanced behind Maerlis and met Jim's gaze. "Do we need to call in help?"

"We have to be close," she said, shaking her head. "If this is starting in the oceans, the Dalsoria must be nearby."

"Where's the next search, Belles?" Jim said. "How far away?"

"The next target on our map is several islands away from here," she said. "Another overnight flight. But we don't want to go that direction. We need to go back to an area we missed."

"What have you found?" Rob grinned like his young cadet self. No matter what else was going on, that smile warmed Jim's heart.

"The seeds for the sea grass, seaweed, all come from a central storage facility. The group here has heard of problems starting in several growing areas, in different seaweed crops. It would be much easier to work from there to infect many places at once."

"Are there caves close by?" Jim said. "I don't remember any from the map."

"A couple of pups from this group tend to explore where they're not supposed to," Nesil said. The other Greponians hissed laughter. "Not exactly unusual for us. They found a cave system with an entrance underwater. Human mappers probably missed it."

"Whoever we're up against didn't," Maerlis said. "The Dalsoria aren't exactly master strategists, not going by what Kayren told us. Whoever's directing them would have a hard time moving them without getting caught."

"Better to put them in the middle of everything," Rob said. "No tourist is going to bother with an underwater cave in the middle of nowhere with hundreds of more interesting diving spots by the resorts. How far away is this seed storage?"

"Three hours fast over the water," Nesil said. "Less than an hour if we fly."

CHAPTER 13

JIM HAD NEVER HAD a clear understanding of how much the equatorial zone had developed around Mossera 4 in the decades he'd lived there. When he'd first arrived and taken his brief tour of Mosserrania, he'd seen mostly resorts and rec complexes on the existing islands ringing the middle of the planet. There were a few half-constructed diving habitats and rumors of more on the way, but not much else.

The vast expanse dedicated to relaxation had seemed like an unimaginable paradise to him so soon after a time of horrible war.

During the brief flight just ahead of the sunset with Rob and Maerlis at his side, the ship passed over dozens of diving or recreation islands, too round and perfect to be natural. They also passed over more aquaculture zones than he could keep count of. Most would be invisible from the water, or to a tourist or miner who didn't know what they were seeing.

Mossera's clear water revealed rows cultivated under the surface that weren't all that different from where he and Rob worked much further north. Some round, some in a standard rectangular grid. The plants flashed from browns to reds, purples to barely visible greens against the sandy seabed.

Knowing the Dalsoria were somewhere nearby, and that whoever controlled them was already active in this rich ocean farmland, only increased his anxiety about stopping the attack before it got worse.

"That's got to be the storage facility." Maerlis pointed dead ahead, drawing Jim's focus from a perfectly square mat of luminescence off to the left. "Those must be constructed pools."

Sharp bright squares and circles stood out against the darkening waters, each nearly as large as the growing fields they'd just passed over. Jim gave up when his count passed thirty, all on one side of a rocky island. He couldn't see how many were hidden by the mountains.

"Isn't this a secured facility?" he said. "They're not just going to let a pleasure craft land close by."

"You'd be right." Rob tapped his breast pocket. "If it weren't for the useful travel auth you secured for us, old man. Scouting for farming expansion, remember?"

"I have a meeting scheduled with the supervisor tomorrow afternoon," Maerlis said. "Have to make sure the species they're growing are compatible with ours."

"Except they don't know what species they're growing," Jim said. "Not any more."

The boat circled past the growing pools and their high concrete edges, settling on the right side of the island. Jim spotted a few more pools in the distance, but not as many on the other side.

"How could Dalsoria be this close to a ConSpace growing facility?" Maerlis said as they headed downstairs to the tanks. "Wouldn't they notice the change in the water?"

"This might be the perfect place," Rob said. "I'm sure those big concrete pools out there go all the way to the bottom, to keep each species isolated. Just like we do in the greenhouses. Then they transfer the crops out to the open ocean. They'd probably be a lot more worried about the water quality inside the pools than out."

"That's what we thought we were doing," Jim said. "The attack made it to our pollen stores already, at least some of them. I hope we're in time to save these crops."

All five Greponians were circling in the tank, growling and barking. They'd always searched during daylight so far, but they were clearly eager to get started.

"If they attack the moving seafood," Maerlis said, gripping Rob's hand, "mollusks and fish, we might not ever be able to stop it. Not if they spawn in the ocean."

Belles and her mighty tail splash pulled Jim's attention away from the nightmare scenario he'd been worried about for days now.

"Nesil and I scouted as soon as we landed. We smell traces of the sweet water we've been seeking."

Nesil bobbed his head, his coppery lightning streaks glinting.

"The plume extends in several directions with the currents, but we think it's coming from the island. Exactly where the cave is supposed to be."

"Do you need to wait until morning?" Jim said, glancing at the portals behind them. They were underwater, but he could see only a trace of sunlight filtering through.

"This search is by smell," Belles said. "And by taste. The question is whether humans can search by night."

"Humans?" Jim said before he could stop himself.

Of course they'd have to be involved in this part. He could ask the Greponians to locate the cave they needed, and maybe identify the Dalsoria. But he couldn't, and would not, allow them to confront whoever was behind these attacks.

"Yes, humans!" Maerlis had already pulled diving equipment down for herself, a gleaming black suit and transparent goggles. "We've let you do all the work long enough."

"We can't…" Rob said, swallowing hard. "I wasn't joking about not being able to swim, Maer."

"Just use one of these," she said. She dropped a larger version of the diving suit at his feet. "You can breathe with the mask, and one of us will tow you. Or you can use the submarine, but that might not make it into the cave."

Rob shook his head, but Jim jumped in before he could speak.

"I'm not the best swimmer myself. We'll all go out in the boat, get as close to the cave as we can. Then we'll know exactly where the cave is instead of having to wander around."

"Yes, this makes sense to us," Belles said. "Waiting for humans to swim would be too slow. We will find the cave, then direct you to it."

Maerlis shook her head, clearly ready to argue. When she caught sight of Rob's pale face and wide-eyed expression, she relented.

"I'll get the boat ready. You two try out the suits, make sure they fit and you know how to use the breather." She tapped her bare foot for a few seconds, then looked at Jim. "Think it may be time to let someone know where we are? What's going on?"

Jim picked up the slick rubbery suit, holding it up against his body. It looked a few sizes too small, but he knew they stretched quite a bit.

"I'll ask the crew to send a message to the leader of the growing facility here. And I'll send a message to one of my buddies in ConSpace Security. Nothing detailed, not yet. But I'll let her know to keep an ear to the ground for us. Or to the water."

Maerlis nodded once, then headed toward the boat docks up front.

"Ready for this?" Jim said. He held the larger suit out toward Rob.

"No. Not even a little. I thought I might get to paddle around before I jumped right into an underwater cave." He gripped one arm of the suit, stretching it between his hands. "I'm not letting her go out there without me, though. You either."

CHAPTER 14

Before Jim or Rob quite managed to get comfortable in the suits but after he'd sent his messages, the Greponians returned in a burst of more ear-piercing squealing. The thickening streams of sweet water led to a cave entrance a few meters below the surface. No signs of guards or defenses, but they hadn't gone all the way inside.

Jim had the clear impression they didn't like it, especially Belles and Nesil, but they'd listened to the humans begging them not to face whatever was in the cave. Their impatience while waiting for the boat to reach the jagged face of the cliff showed even more clearly.

Thanks to the huge pleasure craft's supply of night diving equipment, Jim could watch the Greponians circling the small boat. The close-fitting goggles he, Rob, and Maerlis wore let them see a few meters under the water as well as the rock wall ahead of them. Red-shifted dive lights would help illuminate the cave once they headed inside.

Rob gripped the edge of the small bamblewood boat, staring at his flippered feet more than the open water around them. Jim wished the younger man had admitted he wasn't just unable to swim. Rob was obviously frightened of being in such a small, fast-moving boat, dreading whatever lay ahead.

Jim tried to stop himself from running his fingertips over the emergency beacon the leader of their pleasure craft crew had pressed into his palm, refusing to let him leave without it. The round thumb key wasn't going to fall out of the rubbery inside of the suit's hip pocket, no matter how much he worried about it. One sharp press with his thumb, and they'd have whatever backup the crew could provide.

He kept his own emergency beacon, a souvenir of gratitude for his military service, to himself. Jim had never had to use the slim medallion implanted into an indigo bracelet. He hadn't worn it for longer than he could remember back on Mosslea, but it never left his pocket. He hoped he wouldn't need the direct link to ConSpace Security now or any time in the future.

That hadn't stopped him from fitting the bracelet just under the sleeve of the dive suit before they set out.

Maerlis stood up in front of the boat, where she'd been crouching to talk to Belles. Rob managed to hold out a hand to her when she reached the two men instead of asking her to be careful. Again.

"There's a rock just to the right of the cave where we can anchor, about a meter down. Still no signs of guards or any kind of barrier. We don't know what's inside there, though."

"Think it's big enough for us to fit through?" Rob was finally staring at the rock wall rising above them rather than at his own feet.

"If the Dalsoria are there, someone has to be visiting them," Jim said. "Or something. Otherwise they couldn't get anything in or out for them to modify."

Rob nodded slowly, still gripping the sides of the boat. Maerlis sat beside him, gently turning his face toward hers.

"We'll have five natural swimmers with us, sweetheart. Jim and I will be fine. Would you please stay with the boat in case we need help?"

He let go long enough to brush his fingertips through the water, keeping a tight grip on the other side as he leaned. Jim pretended not to notice Rob's shaking hand.

"I'll go behind you two, okay? You showed me how to use the mask, so I know I can breathe. Just make sure someone knows to pull me back out if I get into trouble."

Maerlis stared into Rob's eyes, then turned to Jim.

"You're a much better swimmer than I am," Jim said. "You stay with Belles, and I'll keep hold of Rob. We'll tell the other Greponians to do the same."

Belles surfaced with two more furry heads close behind her.

"The boat is anchored. None of us can hear anything, but the smell and taste of the water is strong. We're in the right place."

"We're ready." Maerlis turned to Rob again, smiling. "Just remember, breathe normally once you have your mask on. Belles and the others will make sure you're safe."

"We're accustomed to keeping up with humans," Belles said. "Any of us with dive training know you are new to the water."

"Thanks for that." Rob pulled the teardrop-shaped transparent mask up over his nose and mouth. Jim saw his chest rise and fall before he held up both thumbs.

"You're doing great," Maerlis said. She pulled her own mask up, and Jim heard her voice through the speaker built into his diving cap. "We can all speak, and Belles has a transmitter."

She moved to the flattened edge of the boat, grinned at Rob and Jim, then flipped backward into the water. Jim scooted until he was beside the ladder instead, gesturing to Rob to go first.

"I'm right here," he said. "Stay close, and come back out if you need to."

Rob climbed down the ladder and went under the surface. Jim saw two red dive lights flip on. Nothing left to do but jump in himself.

And hope for the best.

CHAPTER 15

THE CAVE WAS MUCH WIDER than Jim feared, leaving room for him and Maerlis to swim side by side. Belles and Nesil went in front, and the other three followed behind Rob. The red lights showed irregular dark rock all around them. No signs of machinery or anything other than a natural cave.

"Light up ahead," Belles said. "Faint, but clear. Someone's in here."

Maerlis darted ahead. Jim touched her foot before she got too far away.

"You're not going to let me go first, are you? Just promise you'll look, not engage. If anything serious is going on, or if there are guards, we back out of here and call in the professionals."

"I got it, Jim. And no, you're not going first. You're too slow."

She joined the two Greponians in front, and they swam out of sight around a bend in the cave.

Jim touched Rob's shoulder, and they moved forward together.

"Check in, Maer," Rob said, his breathing fast in the speaker. "Let me know what's happening."

"Still moving. Turning my dive light off. Definitely something glowing ahead." Several seconds passed, with only her slow, steady breaths. Her voice dropped to a whisper. "There's the surface. Staying back against the cave wall. Hang on."

Jim pointed up ahead. They'd passed the same curve, and he could see the yellowish glow. He turned off his dive light. Rob looked in a circle around and in front of them before he did the same.

"Someone here," Maerlis whispered, almost too soft to understand. "Some*thing*. Two, no, three of them. A whole shelter in here, supplies and all. May have been here for—"

She gasped, and Jim jerked when she yelled.

"In the water! Belles, it's in—"

She yelled again, too loud for Jim to make out the words. Before he could grab Rob, furry bodies passed over both of them. The Greponians gripped both men with their back feet and surged forward.

"Maerlis!" Rob shouted, flailing his arms, knocking into Jim more than moving himself in the water. "What's happening?"

"—got Nesil! Belles, watch out!"

The cave streaked by, growing brighter until Jim's face burst out of the water. Too much noise and motion made it impossible to understand what he was seeing. Rob's bellowing only made matters worse.

"Where are you! Maerlis!"

A huge hand smacked Jim's mask, driving pain into his nose and making him see spots. He caught Rob's wrist and squeezed hard.

"Stop it, Rob! Let me find her!"

Jim yanked his mask and goggles off, holding tight to

Rob. A horrifying, oily thick stench coated his nose and throat. Worse than a spoiling compost pile full of maggots and flies, worse than acres of rotting old Earth battlefields filled with the dead and dying.

A shelf of rock rose up a few meters away. Several lights along the back wall made it hard to distinguish the shapes moving along the edge.

Rob screamed then, trying to jerk his wrist away.

"Something in the water, grabbed at my foot. Maerlis!"

CHAPTER 16

Splashes exploded in front of Jim and Rob, right in front of the shelf.

Maerlis with her arm wrapped around Nesil, trying to drag him out of the water.

Belles pushing from behind, grunting loud enough to make deep ripples.

Neither Maerlis nor the Greponians saw the things waiting along the cave wall.

"Watch out!" Jim let go of Rob and lunged forward, trying to get to Maerlis. Strong paws gripped his waist, nearly throwing him onto the rock.

Jim raised his arms, hoping he looked more threatening than he felt. Hoping he wouldn't throw up before he could protect anyone. Or himself.

"Stay back! Don't get near her!"

The things could have been human if glimpsed through wavy glass, or maybe through watering eyes.

Heads and limbs slumped like melting wax, sickly green and mottled grey.

What should have been eyes were sunken, bruised

looking pits, and irregular gaping holes held space for mouths. He could barely hear the noises coming from the creatures, not with shouting humans and grunting Greponians.

What he heard sounded more like cries from dying artificial babies, a deranged child's toy, than any attempt at communication.

"Maerlis, watch out behind you!" Jim got to his feet, ducking to avoid the low ceiling. "Stay back!"

The things, Dalsoria he guessed, cowered back from his waving arms. But they immediately started moving forward again, oozing and undulating across the cave floor.

"Something got Nesil," Maerlis said, her voice loud but not panicked. "One of them, I think. Rob! Get your head up!"

Jim glanced over his shoulder, long enough to see a violet paw shove his red-faced and choking cadet onto the ledge. He also saw Nesil, kicking and struggling with five limbs.

The sixth limb sank into the middle of what had to be another Dalsoria. This one a horrifying version of a Greponian. Seven limbs more like rotting tentacles, purple and blue and black streaks on sticky, matted fur.

Jim grabbed under Rob's shoulders, hauling him up onto the rock.

"Help me, Rob. Get up, but watch your head."

Rob sputtered and coughed, dragging himself up onto his knees.

"Maerlis…"

"She's fine, Belles is helping her. I need you, right now!"

The three shapes moved forward again, almost close enough reach the water. Jim lunged at them.

"Get closer and we'll kill that one!"

All three turned their sagging faces toward him, unable to

blink but clearly paying attention now. Rob grabbed Jim's hand, pulling until he stood, hands on his knees.

"You understand me," Jim said. The Dalsoria made no reply, but they didn't move, either. He pointed toward Nesil, still twisting and trying to free his limb. "Tell that one to let go. We don't want to hurt any of you."

Three faces flowed around the sides of the heads, pointing more or less toward Maerlis and the Greponians. The crazed, slippery creature holding Nesil's limb lay half in, half out of the water.

"Tell it to let go!" Maerlis yelled. "Now!"

The awful singsong babble started up again, wavering and slipping from one pitch to another. The one holding Nesil responded, sounding like a Greponian struggling to speak through a throat full of sludge.

"What the hell are they?" Rob said, gasping for breath. "Dalsoria?"

"I think so," Jim said. "That one's letting go of Nesil, so they understand us."

Nesil's paw gradually slipped free, making a horribly loud squelch.

"Are you hurt?" Belles said. She moved to pull Nesil toward her.

"No, Belles!" Maerlis reached between the two. "If he's infected, he may be contagious. Nesil?"

"I don't feel hurt." He cradled his paw with the other three. "My foot feels sick, like it wants to vomit."

"Watch that one," Jim said, pointing at the Dalsoria trying to slip back into the water. "Don't touch its belly."

Belles and the other three grabbed the slimy, diseased-looking version of themselves and threw it up onto the rock.

"How do you talk to them?" Jim said, turning toward the fleshy Dalsoria. "The ones who put you here? How do you know what to do next? We promise not to hurt you if you help us. We may even get you out of here."

After a moment, all three faces slipped and turned toward the wall to Jim's right. The sleek comm boxes weren't any kind he'd seen before, but it was clearly human technology. Advanced models, too, much newer than anything Jim had seen on Mossera 4.

"We need to get Nesil out of here," he said. "Maybe you can help him in your lab, Maerlis." He turned back to the Dalsoria. "Do you have anything here now? Something they told you to modify?"

One of them moved toward the back wall of the cave, slouching like a human with no bones to keep them from collapsing. Jim's stomach protested again, but he bit his tongue to force himself to focus.

He stepped over to a wide tank, easily big enough for him and Rob to fit into. Inside swam dozens of fish, all different species. Another tank close by held shellfish, oysters, and other shelled creatures Jim didn't recognize.

The next phase of the attack.

But they still didn't know who was behind all of this.

"Do you have a way to call them?" he said. "The ones who bring things to you? Just show me, don't call them right now."

Another of the humanoid Dalsoria shifted toward the wall with the comm unit. Jim saw its stomach, or whatever it would be called. This one was where a human's chest would be, soft and caved in. The flesh glistened in the low light.

The Dalsoria tapped three soft appendages just below the comm, making a pattern too fast for Jim to recognize.

"Okay, good." He waved toward the middle of the rock shelf. "Get back together now, where we can see you. What do we do now?"

Maerlis pulled herself up onto the ledge, keep clear of the watery Dalsoria crawling toward the other three.

"We have to get Nesil out of here. And we have to call for help. What's in the tanks, Jim?"

"Fish, mollusks. Just what we were afraid of happening next."

"Call them now," Rob said. He dropped to his knees beside Maerlis, hands on her shoulders. Jim thought he wanted to hold a lot more of her than that. "Get back to the boat, call them, and get the hell out of here. They have more than enough to find."

"No, not enough." Belles darted back and forth in front of Nesil, more distressed than Jim had ever seen a Greponian. "Catch who did this. Stop them from doing more."

"Get Nesil back to the big boat," Jim said. "Rob, help Maerlis. Once you're on board, let me know. I'll have the Dalsoria call their handlers. Then I'll alert ConSpace Security."

"You can just do that?" Rob said. "Call them up?"

Jim pulled his dive suit sleeve down, revealing the blue bracelet.

"A little reminder of my military service. Yeah, I can just call them up."

"The dive suit systems won't work inside the caves," Belles said. She'd stopped darting around, but she watched Nesil closely. "Not as far away as the ship. Suma, you wait outside. When Nesil is on board, tell us, then head back yourself. Jim will make his calls. I'll get him out of here."

CHAPTER 17

"Now, Jim," Belles said when they surfaced outside the cave. "We must get Nesil to safety before these attackers show up. They've done more than enough damage."

Jim took a deep breath, letting the fresh, salty air wash the last of the reek of the cave away. He had no way to know how long the Dalsoria handlers would take to arrive, or even what the creatures had said in their message.

None of that mattered, not anymore. They had their proof. They needed help.

His dread of dealing with ConSpace Security didn't matter any more, either.

As soon as his fingertips pressed the medallion, a woman's tinny voice spoke.

"Planetary Security. Name and identity code, please."

Jim rattled off his ancient soldier's credentials without hesitation. He doubted he could have called them to mind before that second.

"James Turhan," the tinny voice said. "Director of Educational Services, Mosslea Academy. Current location, Mosserrania. Secured ConSpace seafood growing facility. Please explain your unauthorized location and your call."

"I…there's been a report of a restricted species. I can confirm the report. Extreme danger to Mossera 4 and all ConSpace operations."

"Please identify the restricted species."

"Dalsoria. Four of them. There's evidence of tampering with our food supplies. Ongoing tampering."

The unit fell silent except for a series of clicks.

A churning hum rose from the opposite side of the island, getting louder and closer.

"Jim," Belles said.

"Please explain your location and how you know of this threat."

"No ma'am. Respectfully, not right now. I'll explain everything to Mossera 4 Command in person, please. I'm requesting an immediate response to the presence of a restricted species."

Belles tugged Jim's arm, dragging him away from the rock. The hum resolved into a powerful motor, and a boat came around the edge of the cliff.

"Jim, we must submerge."

"I hear it. ConSpace Security, situation escalating down here. Immediate physical danger. Please respond to restricted species. Be prepared for armed conflict. We're about to have company."

The motor stopped, and the boat drifted into the same spot where they'd been anchored just a few minutes ago. Belles started pulling Jim backward.

"Breather on," she said, her voice barely carrying over the translator bud. "We must submerge."

Jim shook his head, holding the bracelet closer to his mouth. Hoping the tinny voice wouldn't carry the few meters across the water.

His goggles showed several dark suited figures moving around on the boat.

All of them much bigger than Rob.

All of them armed with some kind of heavy rifle.

"Units dispatched. Can you remain at your location?"

Belles froze, just like everyone on the boat. One of them dropped his rifle and picked up an electric torch. The blinding white beam moved across the water in widening circles.

"No ma'am, too dangerous," Jim whispered. "I'll wear my link for the next few days."

"We will find you. Move to safety immediately."

The light flashed into Jim's eyes. He was too blinded to see anyone pointing rifles his way, but he heard a shouted command.

"Okay, Belles. Get us out of here."

CHAPTER 18

FIVE WEEKS LATER:

Kayren leaned back in her lounger, folding her seven limbs across her leathery abdomen. The Crithien's color had faded from the brilliant magenta of pre-molting back to her normal sky blue. Her latest messy transformation gave her a sixth segment, smaller than the others but complete with a new brain.

She tilted her head from one side to the other, regarding Jim with dozens of glittering compound eyes. He sat calmly in one of her human-specific chairs, looking back at her. Kayren gazed at Rob and Maerlis in turn, sitting close together on her sofa.

After their adventure with the Dalsoria, all three of them were decidedly calmer in the presence of a massive, super-intelligent insect. At least Kayren's genetics were stable, and theirs were in no danger of being altered no matter how intently she stared at them.

"And the Greponian, Belles," Kayren said, her insectile buzzing clear and easy to understand. "She pulled you to safety, Jim?"

"She did. I just about drowned myself, though. I didn't get my breather on in time, so I had to hold my breath most of the way. Not an easy thing at the speed she swims."

Rob shook his head, smiling at his teacher. "You had us scared, old man. Took a couple of good thumps on the chest to get you to cough up all that seawater."

"Yeah, I appreciate that." Jim rubbed at his chest. "Could have done without the cracked ribs, though."

"The spies, they did not pursue you?"

"They got interrupted by Jim's buddies at ConSpace Security," Maerlis said. "We heard their energy rifles blast a few times, then what sounded like an explosion over our heads. A full troop transport, bearing down with heavy arms and thirty soldiers, against seven guys on a boat. Wish I could have seen their faces."

"We can still see their faces," Rob said. "Thanks to Kayren here."

"It seemed the least I could do," Kayren said. "Your actions saved the Mossera System considerable hardship, if not total collapse. I'm sure ConSpace would allow you to attend their galactic court trial even without my influence."

"I'd rather not go, given the choice." Jim finished his beer, then got up to pour more for himself and Rob. Maerlis was still sipping water. "I've had enough of courts and testifying and questions to last five lifetimes."

"Yes, I've reviewed your testimony, Jim." Kayren nodded when Jim offered her more of her own fermented beverage. After seeing the luminescent orange color, he'd decided not to ask questions. "You handled yourself very well for such a serious situation."

"I managed not to get thrown into prison, is that what you mean?" Jim said, laughing. "Junima would still love to see me locked up for dragging her precious pups along on our crazy expedition."

Rob held up his glass, grinning. "I think the only thing that saved any of us was working ourselves half to death getting this new pollination cycle underway in record time. They can't exactly throw us in prison when we're heroes, can they?"

"Especially not when only a handful of us ever knew the real danger." Maerlis touched her glass to Rob's. "Planetwide panic, averted."

Jim held up his own glass before taking a long drink. They'd finished final inspection earlier that day. Pollen from their secured stores, carried in carefully sterilized drones. Fields washed down with great loads of water carried from the oceans to remove as much of the mutated pollen as they could.

So far new fruit was setting on all but a few of the affected species.

They'd have to be vigilant for years, watching for that Dalsoria virus to return. But at least now they understood what they were looking for. And they had an ally in understanding and fighting the problem if it ever did come back.

"We'll have a couple of lean months," Jim said. "Shortages of a few fruits and vegetables. Easy enough to explain one bad season instead of surviving a bad year. We'll get through."

"How is the wounded one faring?" Kayren said.

"Nesil is doing well," Maerlis said. "I was able to arrest the damage to his DNA before it spread beyond his paw. He did lose it, though."

"He would have lost his life if not for you." Rob reached for her hand. "Him and a bunch of other Greponians, probably."

"We don't know what the manipulations would have been," Maerlis said, swatting his hand away. "The Dalsoria might have been improving him for all you know. Should have let them get hold of you."

Kayren picked up a touch screen designed to respond to Crithien limbs.

"That's how you helped Nesil, Maerlis? By studying the Dalsoria?"

"My new guests were quite happy to help once they understood the problem. And once we learned how to adapt the translators to them."

Jim shuddered, trying to hide his reaction. He understood why the creatures couldn't leave, not with their restricted status and the crimes they'd been involved in. Creating a highly secured and tightly controlled habitat for them, deep under Maerlis's lab, seemed like the most humane solution.

They were, after all, innocent of the crimes, acting on human instruction.

"I still don't like you working with them, Maer," Rob said. He sat forward, rubbing his hands against his knees.

"You think I'd pass up the research opportunity of a lifetime?" she said. "Several lifetimes? Thousands of scientists across the known systems would give anything to study the Dalsoria. And I never get close to them, you know that. Thick plas-glass walls, guards everywhere. Dalsoria are very sweet once you get to know them."

"I look forward to meeting them as well," Kayren said. "Perhaps when the galactic trial has concluded. I do wonder what the sentence will be."

"They tried to destroy everything we've built here," Jim said, more sharply than he intended. "All so PittGalactic could swoop in, buy up the Mossera System, and rescue us all. If there's any justice, they'll get a lifetime of hard labor on Mossera 5."

Jim struggled with himself, as he had countless times since his own trial. His friend in ConSpace Security had admitted, to him and in private, that he'd probably made the right choice in not calling them sooner. Any overreaction and resulting panic would have played right into PittGalactic's hands.

He figured he'd admit that much to Maerlis, and maybe Rob. Someday. When all this fuss and bother finally died down.

As the silence stretched out, Rob started fidgeting, then shifting around the same way Maerlis had. Jim recognized the signs from years of experience.

"All right, kid," he said, glad for an excuse to speak up after his outburst. "What are you wanting to say?"

Rob shook his head, staring into the corner for a few seconds. He didn't manage to hide his broad smile. As Jim knew he would, he started talking.

"We…Maerlis and I want to…" Rob's face flushed as red as when Jim first saw the two of them together. "Go ahead, Maer."

"I'm pregnant," she said, throwing her hands up and smiling. "Got confirmation today. We figure it happened sometime during our grand adventure down on Mosserrania. Just like all the tourists and miners, right?"

Jim jumped up and caught the two of them in a hug. He smiled while Maerlis, and even Rob, hugged Kayren as best they could.

"You are well-matched," the Crithien said. "I look forward to welcoming a new member of your family."

"Congratulations don't even come close," Jim said. "I couldn't be happier for both of you."

"I'm glad you feel that way, Jim." Rob looked into Maerlis's eyes, then settled his hand on her belly. She covered it with hers. "I hope you won't mind company on your twilight walks once I'm carrying a fussy baby around half the night."

"You know," Maerlis said, turning back to Jim. "Since none of our parents are here."

"Makes things a little harder." Rob ducked his head and grinned, sending Jim back to his earliest days trying to keep up with him as an unruly cadet. "We were kinda hoping…"

Maerlis took her turn. "If you wanted to…"

"I'd be the luckiest man in the whole system, being a part of this baby's life. Any way you need me to." Jim paused to wipe a tear before it could get away. "That's what Granddads are for."

ABOUT KARI

Kari Kilgore's wanderlust and imagination lead her all over the world on grand adventures. Her heart and family bring her home to her native Appalachian Mountains of Virginia. From that solid base, she and her husband Jason A. Adams bring those adventures to life in fiction.

She hopes the first non-Earth species discovered won't require restrictions. She'd still like to learn everything she can about it either way.

Kari writes science fiction, fantasy, mystery, romance, contemporary fiction, and everything in between, and she's happiest when she surprises herself. She lives at the end of a long dirt road in the middle of the woods with Jason, various house critters, and wildlife they're better off not knowing more about.

The Confidential Adventure Club

For Kari's exclusive free After The End stories and deleted scenes, discounts, early pre-sale releases, adorable pet photos, and a whole lot more not available anywhere else, join us in The Club.

Hope to see you there!

www.KariKilgore.com
www.SpiralPublishing.net
www.ConfidentialAdventureClub.com

ALSO BY KARI KILGORE

I hope you enjoyed reading *Restricted Species* as much as I enjoyed writing it. For more space opera and galactic empire stories, be sure to visit www.DispatchesFromTheGalaxy.com.

For more science fiction from both me and Jason A. Adams, head over to www.SpiralPublishing.net/ScienceFiction.

Be the first to know about release dates and check out more of my fiction across almost every genre at www.KariKilgore.com.

Dispatches from the Galaxy Space Opera Stories:

Restricted Species

The Becalmed

The Garbage Belt

Plurapod Pathogen

The Changes Cascade

Dispatches from the Galaxy: A Space Opera Novella Trio

Near Future Forward (with Jason A. Adams)

The Storms of Future Past Series:

Dreaming the Storm

Joining the Storm

Into the Storm

Fighting the Storm

Sensing the Storm: A Storms of Future Past Prequel

Storms of the Heart: A Storms of Future Past Romance

Storms of Future Past Books One through Four Collection

The Odd Society:

Independent by Means of Magic

Protected by Means of Magic

The Voices through Time Series:

Songs in the Mountain

Secrets in the Land

Walking the Ghosts: A Voices through Time Novella

Novels:

Until Death

The Dream Thief

Hand Me Downs

Protecting Her Own

Novellas:

Legacy of the Land

In the Pines

DNA Never Lies

The Box of Possibilities

Collections:

Fantastic Women: A Dark Fantasy Novella Trio

Fantastic Shorts: Volume 1

Fantastic Shorts: Volume 2

Partners in Romance (with Jason A. Adams)

Fantastic Shorts: Volume 3

Escape into Romance: A Collection of Sweet Beginnings

Stepping Out of Reality: Short Spells of Appalachian Magic

Facing Down Extraordinary: A Series of Ordinary Heroes

Hacking Cybercrime: Dana Sanderson Short Mysteries

Shadows Mountain Deep (with Jason A. Adams)

Investigations Beyond Belief: The Initial Adventures of Deb Powers: Otherworldly PI

Passages in the Real World: Six Stories of Life's Transitions

Fantastic Side Trips: Side Characters Take Center Stage

A Kaleidoscope of Cat Tales: Five Stories of Cats and People Who Love Them

A Tapestry of Holiday Tales: Winter Adventures from the Odds and Endings Bookstore

Uncommon Holidays: A Different Side of the Season (with Jason A. Adams)

Aunties Among Us: Five Tales of Fabulous Women

Four-Legged Heroes: When Pets Rescue People